Star-nosed
n

T0364345

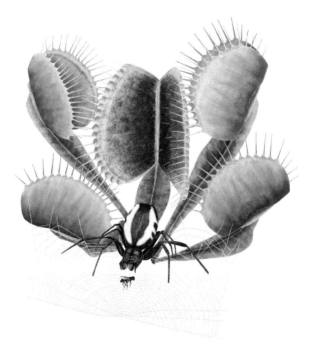

Written by Dom Conlon

Illustrated by Rhian Davie

Collins

Contents

Land

Sea

Sky

Land

Venus fly trap

I like to eat things
which fall into my trap,
says the spider.

Snap, says the trap.

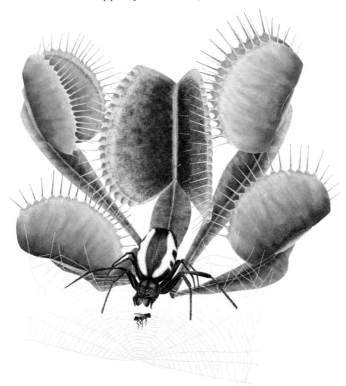

Panda ant

Panda ant is really a wasp
who hides her sting
while living disguised as an ant.

Maybe she stole panda's jumper
which had shrunk in the wash,
and then tumble-dried in Chile's sandy air.

But she's wingless, not harmless,
and whistles her warnings
while searching for nests to lay eggs in

like poisonous gifts
you won't even see until
they've hatched into tiny killers.

Is she cute and cuddly or
small and deadly?
Don't believe the things you see.

Dragon fruit

They must fall from outer space –
no other place could even think of these.

Grown on the stem of an exploding star,
and wrapped in the skin of a meteor

they're myths and maths all in one
a succulent story, a freeze-frame fireball.

Catch one, wish upon one, slice one in two.
Discover a cloud through which a crowd

of alien eyes stare back at you.

6

Pangolin

A pangolin is ...

... a sink full of dirty plates
dreaming of being a dragon.

... a wrinkled old fisherman
casting his line in a dry pond.

... a desert mole
disguised as a junkyard.

... a dusty old wreck
crashed on a sandy shore.

... the earth
stretching its spine.

Saiga antelope

In lands between mountains
before stories began
when ice lay thick all around,
these antelope loped
like double-horned unicorns.

With floppy noses they fed on the grass
at the foothills of the Kazakhstan mountains.
And over the years their numbers declined
growing fewer like the vanishing snow.

That's how their story might have ended.

But slowly and surely
their numbers returned
with help from the people
who once hunted them down
and the saga of saiga goes on.

Phantastic leaf-tailed gecko

You look at her and wonder how,
how can anything on Earth look that way –
a leafy Rapunzel in a tree tower –
hanging stick-still as she tries
not to be noticed among
the carnival colours of Madagascar.

Until she opens her mouth,
fire-bright and shrill as a sharpening knife,
and everyone notices –
like that time you said something
you shouldn't have.

Star-nosed mole

If you saw him walking backwards
you'd think he was a mole being
chased by an octopus
or an octopus
dragged forward by a mole.

A push-me, pull-me,
fat-fingered face who is happy
underground or underwater.
Sightless but using his nose
to see through smell.

Like sniffing a scarlet rose
and seeing the entire day
in your mind.

Glass frog

Like a drop of morning dew on a leaf
the glass frog squats, thumb-thick,
beside the wavy hair of rivers
that run through
the cloud forests of Central America.

Hiding by hiding nothing
he's all heart and lungs and blood and
this green world stares right through him
seeing only the blue hummingbird
drinking from the red creeper's leaves,
or the giant land snail leaving slimy trails
while army ants march on.

Through that invisible skin
the blood pumps through his veins
and he sits here watching for frog flies.
Those flies want to lay their eggs in his eggs –
like tiny full stops looking to end
the sentence of his children's lives.

Sea

Feather star

Even the sea whispers,
and Feather star catches its words
as it walks along winding paths,
on wispy legs,
as though a plant one day,
having had enough of home,
chose to pull up its roots
and tell all its stories
to the wrigglers and stragglers
among the sponges and corals
of someone else's garden.

Blobfish

Dragged up out of the sea,
a thousand metres out of its depth,
it looks like a teardrop
mixed with snot and called
the ugliest animal alive –
a globfish, a slobfish –
but what do they know?

Swim down to its deep-sea home,
where darkness is the tightest hug
you've ever had,
and see it –
perfectly formed
to be itself.

The Great Barrier Reef

Sunk beneath the waves, the reef is
a refuge wrapped in a sea,
a shanty of colourful coral.
There are clownfish and porpoises,
dolphins and hawkfish,
turtles, wrasses and sharks.

It's a rainbow retreat
where the dugongs dive,
where sponges foam from the rocks.
And no one is lonely, and no one's
an island, and no one's adrift
like a boat.

The reef is a refuge wrapped in a sea
where everyone's life plays a part.

Leafy sea dragon

All flutter and no fire
the leafy sea dragon flies like a flag
over the ruins of the coral reef.

He fights no knights,
strikes fear only in plankton,
and guards just the treasure
of his eggs until they are born.

Those who would hunt him
leave the world poorer.
Those who protect him
enrich the sea.

Wobbegong

The wobbegong is a carpet shark,
tassel-faced scrag ends of rug
saved from the bin to cover
the ocean's dusty floor.

You'll find it lying still
until

with teeth like darning needles,
it shakes itself
to attack.

Sea anemones

In the calm sandpit of the ocean
gardens of baby sunrises play,
waving their rays at the blue sky above.

In nursery-bright colours
they seem so peaceful, clinging
to the safety of a rock – or floating
between the currents, but

even the water can't dampen
the fiery poison they hold in their hugs.

So do not fall prey
to their innocent look.

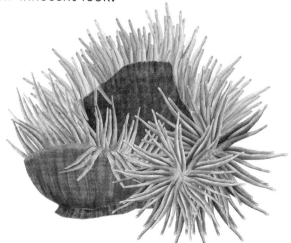

Glass octopus

Oil-black, space-silent, sleep-deep –
here in the deep dark depths of the sea,
    ghosts glide through graveyards
    and the wrecks of long-dead whales
give up their dreams.

Then there,
like the outline of smoke, she drifts,
and rows of dots on her body
glow like a procession of candles
remembering daylight. Watch.
Under her transparent skin
a hundred tiny eggs wait to be born.

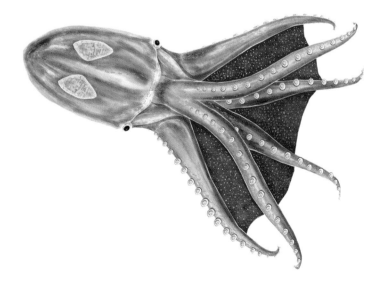

Fangtooth

The dog a hurricane chooses to guard its house.
The cage a safecracker hides her jewels in.
The storm thunder hides under the bed from.

Fangtooth is all tooth and terror
in a tiny tank of scale and spine
swallowing prey in one bite
and angrily glaring around
bumping into others
just to start fights.

Sky

Clouds

A cloud tells the story of how
hot and cold air meet.

It is countless drops of water
standing together or a puddle
waiting to fall.

But to those looking up there's more
to a cloud than science can say.

It's a face looking on or a hand
reaching down – a monster, a bike
or a heart.

A cloud is our worries, our dreams,
and our hopes – it's the story
of our quietest thoughts.

Superb bird-of-paradise

OK. We get it. Superb. Paradise. Bird.
No point comparing them
to the otherworldly colour the sky turns
after a hot day playing by the river when
flocks of birds settle behind velvet reeds.

No point writing how the males compete
for the females' attention
by dancing like fireworks popping
and sweeping among cheering trees.

No point. They're superb. They're paradise.
They don't need more words, but we do.
So use yours to tell everyone you know
and save them from ever dying out.

Haring ibon

Wingspan wide as a parent's open arms
with a hundred children to hug
the eagle of the Philippines
was here before the first humans
stepped on the islands
fifty thousand years ago.

Nothing escapes their eagle-eye view,
forests are their kingdom, love is their home,
and each couple partners for life.

Teddy bear bee

Hey there, teddy bear
all on your own,
why build a nest
just for yourself?

Hey there, teddy bear
all on your own,
making all that room
just for your eggs.

Hey there, teddy bear
all on your own,
get on with your life,
I'll leave you alone.

Rainbow

After the morning rain
had swept the streets
with a fine broom,
the sun stepped out
from behind the clouds
and scattered and splattered
across the sky
all the colours it could see
for the rain to tidy away
later.

Shoebill

He's like a child who forgot
to plan for fancy-dress day,
digging into the wardrobe
only to find all that was left
were dusters for feathers
and an old wooden shoe
for a beak.

Saying nothing
he trudges to school
like a lonely raincloud,
to stand in the playground
where all the other birds
are dressed like royalty.
There he glares
in ruffled rage.

Flying possum

By day you'll find her rug-snug
and rolled up tight, sleeping through
the day until the sun has set.
She wakes, eyes like black pearls
lit by a red moon, fur two sizes too big,
baby in her pouch and claws creeping
and scratching along the branches
until she runs she leaps she
flies
and her body is a carpet carried by the wind
free just to be ...

Isn't the air exciting?
Isn't being alive amazing?

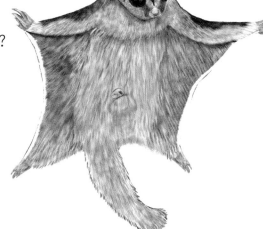

Frigatebird

Ahoy! Sky-lubber! Avast ye Birdy!
Scourge of the high Caribbean clouds!
Your menacing black ship of a body looms
and your crimson sail of a pouch billows
beneath a sharp-hooked cutlass beak
to strike terror in gulls and ospreys
as you steal their treasure
of squid, crab, turtle and jellyfish.
You shake them to the bones
as you rattle your battle cry.
Watch out world, listen and flee,
from the pirates of sky and sea.

Land, sea and sky

Land

"a sink full of dirty plates"

"a leafy Rapunzel
in a tree tower"

"you'd think he was a mole being
chased by an octopus"

Sky

"Wingspan wide as
a parent's open arms"

"your crimson sail of
a pouch billows"

"He's like a child who forgot
to plan for fancy-dress day"

Sea

"like the outline of smoke, she drifts"

"gardens of baby sunrises play"

"the reef is a refuge
wrapped in a sea"

31

Ideas for reading

Written by Jonny Walker
Specialist Teacher and Educational Consultant

Reading objectives

- make links between poems and children's own life experiences
- understand how poets use simile and metaphor
- understand how poets use alliteration

Spoken language objectives

- ask relevant questions to extend their understanding and knowledge
- use relevant strategies to build their vocabulary
- articulate and justify answers, arguments and opinions
- give well-structured descriptions, explanations and narratives for different purposes, including for expressing feelings

Curriculum links: Geography: Locational knowledge and Place knowledge; Science: Plants and animals, including humans

Interest words: disguised, saga, transparent

Talk before reading

- Look at the cover together and read the blurb on the back cover. Explain that this is a book of poems about amazing and unusual things in nature. Ask children what they think is the most amazing living thing they already know.
- Look at the image on the cover and discuss what makes the star-nosed mole amazing and unusual, and why children think it might have that name.

Support personal responses

- Take time to discuss the poems after you have read them. Use the following questions or ask your own.
  - Which poem did you like most in the collection, and why?
  - Which poem is the most enjoyable for you to read aloud?
  - Do any of the poems capture how you feel about yourself? (*For example, I am a bit like a blobfish; I am like a different person when I am back where I belong and feel safe.*)
  - Did you enjoy exploring *Star-nosed Mole*? Why, or why not?